# I Want My Puppets!

Licensed by The Illuminated Film Company
Based on the LITTLE PRINCESS animation series © The Illuminated Film Company 2008.
Made under licence by Andersen Press Ltd., London
'I Want My Puppets!' episode written by Rachel Murrell.
Producer Iain Harvey.  Director Edward Foster.
© The Illuminated Film Company/Tony Ross 2008.
Design and layout © Andersen Press Ltd, 2008.
Printed and bound in China by C&C Offset Printing.
10  9  8  7  6  5  4  3  2  1
British Library Cataloguing in Publication Data available.

ISBN: 978 1 84270 767 8 (Trade edition)
ISBN: 978 1 84939 691 2 (Riverside Books edition)

# I Want
# My Puppets!

Tony Ross

Andersen Press · London

Scruff and Puss took their places. It was time for the puppet show to begin.

"I hope the Big Bad Wolf won't eat me," said the Little Princess in a squeaky fairytale voice. The story was Little Red Riding Hood, but she was just practising for now.

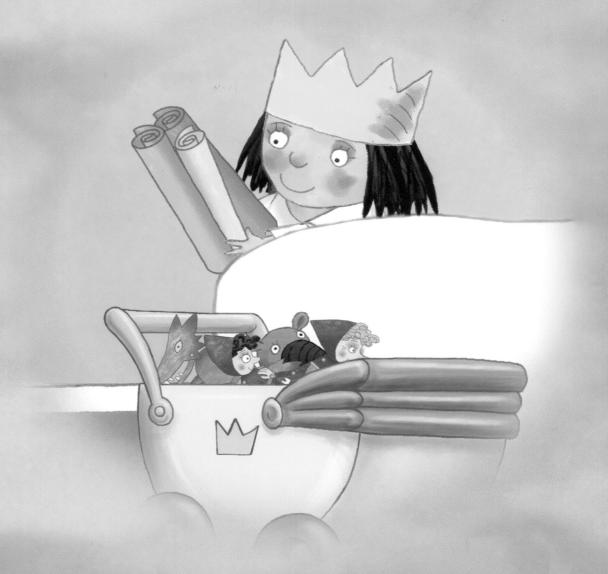

After a while, the Little Princess crawled out from behind
the bed.
"I better go and check my puppet theatre is ready."
She piled all the puppets, posters and tickets into her pram
and wheeled it outside.

"Da-ad!" bellowed the Little Princess. "Where's my puppet theatre?"
The King woke up with a jump. "Um…is tomorrow all right?"
"But I need it now," frowned the Little Princess.
"Poppet," soothed the King. "I can't do it on my own."

The Queen arrived at just the right moment.

"I'll help you!"

The Little Princess giggled and nodded.

She had other things to do.

# "There!"

The Little Princess's theatre poster looked tremendous. "What's this?" asked the General.

"It's my show," announced the Little Princess, handing him a ticket. "Wow!" replied the General. "We'll come, won't we, Nessie?"

But when the Little Princess held up her favourite puppets to show him, the tangled dolls slipped out of her hands and straight into a muddy puddle.

"Hello!" cried the Maid.
The Little Princess scooped up
the puppets and shoved them back in
the pram.
"Will you come to my show?" she asked.
 "The General's coming…"
The Maid blushed. "Oh! Well I'll see what
I can do."

The Little Red Riding Hood tickets were going like hot cakes. "Will there be drinks and nibbles?" asked the Prime Minister. The Little Princess thought for a second. "Of course!"

In the kitchen, the Chef tutted and
shook a saucepan.
"Huh! I'm reduced to making popcorn!"
"I need more!" cried the
Little Princess. "We've got to have enough!"
She squeezed more toffee sauce into her
mixing bowl and kept stirring.

"Naughty," sighed the Chef.

The Little Princess was enjoying herself so much that she didn't notice that gloopy sauce and popcorn were being splattered all over the pram.

Things were shaping up in the garden too.

"That corner is a bit lop-sided, dear," pointed out the King.

"It's perfectly all right," snapped the Queen. "It just needs some curtains."

The Little Princess gasped. "It's lovely!"
The King dropped the puppet theatre into the
sticky pram.
"Here we are, poppet. Be careful now!"

"It's nearly showtime!" screeched the Little Princess.
"Where's the popcorn?"
The Chef came out of his kitchen. *"Voilà!"*
A big bowl of popcorn was plopped on to the pram.

"Thank you!" cried the Little Princess.
A queue of theatre-goers was starting to form outside the living-room. But as the Little Princess pushed past, the pram crashed into the wall with a bang and one of the puppets fell out!

"Oh no!" frowned the Little Princess.
She picked up the poor puppet and tossed her back
into the pram.

By the time the Little Princess had prepared the living-room for the performance, the whole household had joined the queue. "Ladies and Gentlemen," she announced. "The show will begin in…one minute!"

As they waited outside, the audience got more and more excited.
"I hope it's a love story," giggled the Maid.

"Aaaagghh!" yelled a voice from inside.

Everybody hushed at once. "The show is off!" shrieked the
Little Princess. "There will be no show today!"
The King looked at the Queen. "Come on, dear. We'd better see what
the matter is."

The King and Queen found the Little Princess sobbing on a chair.
# "All my puppets are broken!"
"Well you know what they say," said the Queen. "The show must go on!"

The Little Princess stopped crying and had a think. Then, quick as a flash, she dived off the armchair and undid the King's shoe.

"Can't stop to explain!" she cried. "I've got a show to do!"

Once she'd borrowed a few more socks, the little Princess tore
round the castle fetching some other things.
"I need glue from Dad's study," she giggled. "And buttons from
Mum's dresser."
Then it was time to get busy.

Just as the crowd started to wander away, the Little Princess
was back.
"Everything's on again!" she beamed. "Please have your
tickets ready!"

Everybody took their seats. It was very exciting.

"Shhh!" warned the Admiral.

"Ladies and Gentlemen! Cat and Dog!" cried the Little Princess.

"The show is about to begin."
The audience gasped as the King clicked on his torch and
shone it down onto the puppet stage.

The Chef flicked off the ceiling light, and the Little Princess took her place underneath the puppet theatre.

"Once upon a time," she began. "There was a little girl whose name was Little Red Riding Sock!"

"That's my sock!" gulped the Prime Minister.

The crowd shushed him impatiently.
The Little Princess carried on. "She had
a granny who was poorly…"

It was the best puppet show the castle had ever seen.

"So Little Red Riding Sock and her granny lived happily ever after," announced the Little Princess at last. "The end."

The crowd gave the puppeteer a thunderous round of applause.
"Bravo!" cried the Gardener.
"Hurrah for Little Red Riding Sock!" cheered the Maid.

"Hurrah for the Little Princess!"